Selim-Hassan the Seventh

and The Wall

Contents

Written by Vivian French

Illustrated by Tim Stevens

 Collins

Selim-Hassan the Seventh

Chapter 1

Selim-Hassan the Seventh lived in Pushnapanjipetal, which is and was famous for nothing at all, except for the extreme hairiness of all the men who lived there. Selim-Hassan's father was the village barber. Every day he soaped and lathered and foamed the beards of the men of the village and then, with eight swift swoops of his shining silver razor, shaved them so smoothly that their skin felt like the softest silk.

"Look in the mirror," Selim-Hassan's father would say. And the customer would peer at himself in Selim-Hassan's splendid gilt-edged mirror, decorated with golden roses, and nod.

"You are right, Selim-Hassan the Sixth. It is indeed the finest shave that I have ever had."

3

Selim-Hassan's grandfather had been a barber. So also had his great-grandfather, his great-great-grandfather and his great-great-great-grandfather. Each of them in turn had practised and refined the art of shaving from twelve swift swoops of the shining silver razor to eleven, from eleven to ten, from ten to nine. Each of them in turn had passed on their skills and knowledge to their grateful oldest son.

Selim-Hassan the Seventh was different. He did *not* want to be a barber. He was not in the least grateful when his father showed him how to sharpen the razors on a wetted stone. He was not at all grateful when he was given the opportunity to sweep up the curls and whiskers on the shop floor. He was positively rude when a customer asked him to pass him a hot towel.

Selim-Hassan's father grew anxious. "Could it be," he asked Selim-Hassan's mother, "that our son takes after his great-great-great-great-grandfather?"

Selim-Hassan's mother rolled her eyes. "I pray that it isn't so," she said.

Selim-Hassan's great-great-great-great-grandfather, the first Selim-Hassan, had been a pirate. He had sailed the oceans of the world wrecking ships and collecting thousands of shiny objects so that he could see his reflection any time he felt the need. It was Selim-Hassan's great-great-great-great-grandfather who had brought the splendid gilt-edged mirror, decorated with golden roses, back to the village in a treasure chest, together with the silver razors. He never used the razors; he spent his days admiring his wonderfully luxuriant black and curly beard in the splendid gilt-edged mirror and singing loud piratical songs.

When Selim-Hassan the Seventh began to ask questions about this less than illustrious ancestor, his father shook his head. "He was not a man to be proud of," Selim-Hassan the Sixth said firmly. "It is not a good thing to be a thief. You, my son, will not be like him. Our family has been waiting for you for seven generations. You will be famous for being the first among us ever to achieve the perfect shave with only seven swift swoops of the silver razor." And Selim-Hassan the Sixth smiled hopefully at the Seventh.

Selim-Hassan the Seventh shuffled his feet and said nothing. He found his lessons in soaping and lathering and foaming tedious. He much preferred to slip away and play marbles with his friends under the shady palm trees by the well.

 # Chapter 2

Days and weeks and months went past.
Selim-Hassan's father began to teach him the art
of shaving, and Selim-Hassan the Seventh found
that even more boring than soaping and
lathering. At least when he was slapping white
foam on to a customer's face he could flick the
lather high in the air and catch it on the end of
his nose, or send a fleet of bubbles floating out
of the window to sparkle in the sunshine.

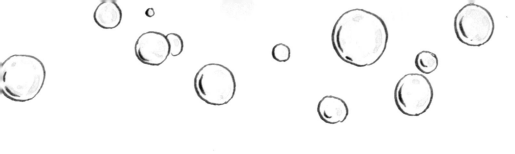

When he was bent over a whiskery chin holding a sharp gleaming silver razor he had to concentrate extremely hard. His father continually told him that it was not good for business to send customers out of the shop dripping globs of blood. Selim-Hassan pulled a face at his father's back and invented his own ways of putting off the time when he would have to take his place as the village barber.

As the weeks went on, the long queue of young men, old men, fat men and thin men outside the barber's shop grew shorter. Some days there were only three or four customers. Men in the village were growing beards for the first time in living memory; day by day more and more whiskers and moustaches and beards could be seen. The barber wrung his hands in despair. He begged Selim-Hassan to try harder, but Selim-Hassan the Seventh just went on flicking his marbles in the air and catching them.

The day before Selim-Hassan's fourteenth birthday was a particularly bad day. Selim-Hassan tipped dirty water over the first customer's new white shirt. He dropped the soap and the second customer slipped and cracked his head on the porcelain sink. The towels he brought for the third customer were so hot that the man leapt out of the chair screaming. He spilt foam all over the floor. He blew bubbles out of the window instead of sweeping up, and he blunted two of the shining silver razors by sharpening them upside down.

"Selim-Hassan," said his father. "You will stay here tonight in the shop after we close. You will sweep the floor and clean it and polish until it shines … and you will not come home until your tasks are done."

Selim-Hassan sighed. "If you say so, Father," he said, and blew another bubble.

13

Chapter 3

When Selim-Hassan was alone in the shop he picked up the broom, and then put it away again. "There's plenty of time for that," he thought, and sitting himself down in the customer's chair he took a couple of marbles out of his pocket and began flicking them this way and that. He looked at himself in the splendid gilt-edged mirror decorated with golden roses, and winked.

Suddenly ...

Clatter clatter! The marbles fell to the floor. Selim-Hassan's eyes popped wide open as he stared at the splendid gilt-edged mirror. Something was happening to his reflection ... something very strange. His hair was growing. His nose was growing. His eyes were deepening ... and lines were appearing on his forehead. His chin sprouted stubble ... then whiskers ... then a full-blown black and curly beard. A golden earring shone brightly in his left ear.

Selim-Hassan clutched at his own ears – there was nothing there. He felt his chin. It was still smooth. He had no beard. He stared transfixed at the mirror. The bearded reflection inside the gilt-edged frame stared back, and then spat loudly. Selim-Hassan's heart jumped into his mouth as a slimy wet blob landed by his foot.

"So!" growled the reflection. "YOU are Selim-Hassan the Seventh!"

Selim-Hassan nodded. He couldn't say a word. His mouth was as dry as dust.

The reflection began to chuckle. "Well well well! After all these generations of mealy-mouthed hard-working lily-livered barbers, I finally find a descendant who takes after ME!"

"Er ..." Selim-Hassan's voice quavered. "Er ... who are you?"

The reflection raised an eyebrow. "Me? Why, Selim-Hassan the First, of course. And delighted to have the opportunity of meeting such a nasty little hairless worm as you. Oh, yes, my boy! You may think you have ideas – but just you wait!"

Selim-Hassan the Seventh began to shake.

"I'm not all bad," he said.

Selim-Hassan the First roared with black-toothed laughter. "Why," he said, "yesterday you nearly cut the spicemixer's throat!"

Selim-Hassan gulped. He thought that nobody had seen the moment when his hand slipped. The wound had, luckily, been only a minor one.

"And," his piratical ancestor went on, "I've seen you slide soap up the schoolmaster's nose."

Selim-Hassan felt himself begin to blush.
It had been fun watching the schoolmaster
sneeze and sneeze and sneeze ... and he had
only done it once. Or was it twice?

"Four times," said the pirate, reading his
mind. "And the baker found a bald patch
shaved on the top of his head. The gravedigger
went home with only one eyebrow. The butcher
had foam in his ears and couldn't hear for a
week ... and THAT is why they have all
decided to go away and grow beards.

Soon every man in the village will do the same ... and your mother and father will starve. And ..." Selim-Hassan the First reached out a long arm and whacked his great-great-great-great-grandson on the back ... "I have plans. GREAT plans! I'll teach you to be a pirate, my boy. We'll raze this village to the ground – and then we'll go to sea! Oh, I've been watching and waiting for this day for a long long long time."

Then to Selim-Hassan the Seventh's complete and utter horror his great-great-great-great-grandfather swung a stout leg over the edge of the frame and began to squeeze himself through, cursing terrible curses as he did so.

Chapter 4

Selim-Hassan's stomach was churning, and his mind was racing. How could he stop this terrifying ancestor of his from wrecking his father's shop ... and the whole village? He didn't want to be a pirate. Water made him ill. And it was one thing to play a few tricks on his father's customers – but to leave his family starving? To raze the village to the ground? Selim-Hassan the Seventh felt weak at the knees.

Meanwhile, his ancestor was grunting and straining to heave his huge shoulders through the gilt-edged frame. "Here, worm," he snarled. "Help me!"

A wild thought leapt into Selim-Hassan's mind. He leant forward. "I hope you're bringing your sword, great-great-great-great-grandfather," he said. "And don't forget your treasure chest!"

The massive figure of the pirate stopped for a moment, puffing hard. "My sword!" he said.

"And the treasure chest," said Selim-Hassan. "We'll need that!"

Selim-Hassan the First swore a string of very nasty oaths, and began heaving himself backwards. Selim-Hassan the Seventh held his breath as the shoulders squeezed away ... and the leg followed. There was a sound of ripping cloth, an oath, and the frame was clear.

Selim-Hassan the Seventh rushed towards the mirror. He tugged and pulled, but it was firmly fixed to the wall. Gasping from his efforts, Selim-Hassan stepped back.

Immediately the furious face of his great-great-great-great-grandfather was in front of him. His eyes were blazing, and his blackened teeth were fixed in a terrible snarl. "Try and get rid of me, would you?" boomed the pirate, and he glared at Selim-Hassan. "Just you wait, little worm, just you ..."

Thwack! A marble hit the pirate in the middle of his forehead. His eyes bulged, and he roared such an enormous roar that the gilt cracked and the golden roses splintered.

Thwack! Another marble hit him on the end of his nose. The pirate roared again, and flung his sword out of the mirror straight at Selim-Hassan, but ...

Splat!

Selim-Hassan the Seventh, well used to dodging his father's arm, ducked, twisted, and shot his last marble straight into Selim-Hassan the First's wide open mouth. Selim-Hassan the First choked, swallowed, hiccupped twice – and disappeared.

Selim-Hassan the Seventh collapsed on the chair. He hardly dared to look in the once-splendid gilt-edged mirror, but when at last he lifted his head and gave a quick glance all he could see was the usual reflection of the barber's shop … reflected in a thousand thousand tiny pieces. The mirror was shattered.

It was a long time before Selim-Hassan's father forgave him for breaking the splendid gilt-edged mirror decorated with golden roses. It wasn't until Selim-Hassan the Seventh shaved the spicemixer with exactly seven swift swoops of his shining silver razor that his father finally stretched out his arms and called him "My son!" once more.

The spicemixer felt his chin, and peered at his reflection in the rather ordinary wooden mirror. "Selim-Hassan the Seventh," he said. "This is the VERY finest shave that I have ever had."

Selim-Hassan the Seventh bowed and smiled, and laid a delightfully warm towel on the spicemixer's chin. He never even glanced at the creaky floorboard by the door. There was no need for anyone else ever to know that under the floorboard were seven glass marbles and a pirate's cutlass.

The Wall

Chapter 1

I was always aware of the wall. Even when I was a tiny girl child strapped to my grandmother's back I would stare and stare at it as we rode past. It was so high! Twelve men standing on each other's shoulders couldn't reach the top ... a monstrous barricade of mud and stone and rock and pebbles. When I was old enough to listen, my brothers told me tales of snakes and dragons and terrible flesh-eating monsters that lived on the other side, and I was glad of its size and strength. It stormed out from the mists where the sun rose in the morning and stretched across my whole world, and was only lost to view in the shadows where the sun set at night. Sometimes, when we moved to the higher ground, I could see it marching over the mountains. It must, I thought, go on for ever.

At first I thought the wall was like the earth, or the trees, or the moon ... something that had always been there. It was only as I grew older that I began to understand that it had been built by men. But who? And why? And gradually I realised something else. The wall made my father angry. To me that seemed the strangest thing of all. Didn't the wall give shade to the horses when the midsummer sun was blazing down? Didn't it mark, clearly and emphatically, the end of the lands where we were safe? When I slipped away from the tents to go walking on my own I was never lost. The wall was always there to show me the way back to wherever we had set up our camp that night. In places it twisted away from being the long straight line that snaked across the grassy plains. When the winter winds were howling and raging we could move our tents close against it and avoid the worst of the cutting icy teeth of the North. I was glad of the shelter of the wall and so was Grandmother Pearl, but my brothers laughed.

"When the old one dies we'll never come near the wall again," they boasted. "And you, Little Rabbit – you must learn to bear the wind in winter and the sun in summer, or you'll never be a true daughter of the horse herders."

I wasn't sure I wanted to be a true daughter if it meant I had to freeze in the winter and scorch in the summer, but I didn't say so. My brothers were too big.

I went on wondering about my father's anger. I never asked him. He was the kind of man who told you what to do, not the sort of man to discuss feelings. The only time he ever talked gently was when he was calming a frightened horse. Sometimes I thought my grandmother and I would have had an easier life if we'd had four hooves and a mane and tail. But maybe not. When my father cracked his long leather-thonged whip, every horse in the herd – even the raw-boned youngsters – did exactly as he told them. Me too. He was far quicker to beat me than he was to beat the silly little foals with their fluffy coats and wobbly legs. Foals grew up to be brood mares and stallions that he could sell for pieces of gold or silver. Me? I was Little Rabbit, and would never amount to anything. Even though I was wiry and strong I was only a girl. It was my duty to walk behind my father, tend the fire, sweep the tents, bake the bread, and look after Grandmother Pearl.

33

Chapter 2

Why didn't I ask Grandmother Pearl the questions
that filled my head? All the questions about the
wall? I did, sometimes ... but she never answered.
She was old – very old. I think perhaps she was
my mother's grandmother, or maybe even older,
and her mind floated free like the clouds in the
sky. When my mother died she looked after me,
but even then she sometimes thought I was one
of her own daughters ... all of whom had died
long ago. I was sorry that she never answered
my questions, but I listened open-mouthed when
she told me her stories – wonderful stories of
strange places, and a strange people who lived a
different life from us.

"They do not move from place to place," Grandmother Pearl told me. "They have houses. The houses are made of wood, and of stone. The people who are rich live with many beautiful things. Their clothes are made of the softest silk. The silk shimmers and shines. It is embroidered with butterflies and flowers and wonderful birds. There are little whispering rivers. Gardens with snow-white and rose-pink petalled trees. The old ..." and here Grandmother Pearl would sometimes give a little sideways glance at my father "... are treated with veneration. They sit and talk, or play music. Some look at the words of poetry painted on to sheets of thin parchment."

My father, if he was paying any attention at all, would snort loudly at this story. "Foolishness!" he would shout. "Nonsense! How can words be painted? Idiocy!"

Grandmother Pearl took little notice of my father's furious interruptions. "When death comes," she went on, "they are dressed in coats made of pieces of precious jade. They are laid to rest in a funeral house for the dead. Horses and servants are placed beside them. Then the houses are closed up, but they are always cared for. They are cared for by the dead one's children, and their children's friends. They respect the houses of their ancestors ... where they belong ..." And then she would sigh and mutter a few words that I couldn't understand, and say nothing more for a long time.

Chapter 3

The first time Grandmother Pearl told me about the funeral houses I stared at her. What did she mean? How could anyone shut horses inside such a place? But she went on telling the story over the years, and gradually I understood that these were not real horses. They were made of clay, and so were the figures of the servants. Once, when I was nine or ten summers old, I found a little clay and began to try and model a horse for myself, but my oldest brother found me and beat me soundly for wasting time.

"Grandmother fills your head with nonsense!" he yelled at me. "What do you need to know of land stealers? When the old one dies and we throw her over the wall we'll teach you what happens to little girls who listen to rubbish – or maybe we'll throw you over too! You can keep her old bones company!"

"WHAT?" I tried to wriggle away, but he held me too tightly. "What do you mean, throw Grandmother over the wall? There are snakes there! And monsters! You told me!"

It was the first time I had ever surprised my oldest brother. He actually stopped beating me, and stared.

"Little Rabbit!" he said at last. "You mean you don't know?"

"Know what?" I asked, rubbing my shoulders.

"You don't know that Grandmother Pearl was born one of them? A Han? One of the Han emperor's people? It was the Hans who stole our land! The evil ones who built the wall so we can't ride our horses over OUR southern hills and plains!" My brother shook his head at me. "Didn't you ever wonder why we keep so close to this monster, this stone snake, this devil's pile of rock and stone?"

"No," I said. I couldn't tell him that I thought the wall was for warmth, and shelter ... and even safety.

"All women have weak brains," my brother growled. "The old woman wants to go back to the land of her birth. Your mother promised her she would be buried there." He glared at me as if it was all my fault.

"And our father will keep that promise ... even though it'll mean death for him if he's seen on the wall. And so we wait. I believe she stays alive to spite us! But when she does die – then it's over the wall with her, and away we'll go! We'll take the horses where the grass grows deep and strong, and NEVER ride here again." He clenched his fist. "Not, that is, until one day all of us beyond the wall come together ... and break it down and take back what is ours!" And his eyes glittered as if he was seeing a vision of the future. It made me shiver, so he beat me some more to make me warm.

Chapter 4

Perhaps my brother was right. Perhaps I was
weak in my brain. After he had left me I sat still,
and thoughts whirled round in my head. So –
Grandmother Pearl came from the other side of
the wall. There were people there – not snakes, or
dragons, or monsters. And her stories ... surely
this meant they were all true? I went on sitting
until the moon came up, and the wall shone
above me as if it was built of blocks of silver.

It was then that I decided. I was going to climb the wall. I was going to climb the wall, and take Grandmother Pearl with me. I would find someone to care for her; someone who would treat her as she wished to be treated. And I would take her before she died, so that she would know that she had come home at last.

I began to watch as we moved from one grazing place to another, watching the wall almost as if it was a living thing. I looked for rough places, weaknesses, places where the reeds that bound the mortar together had dried and fallen away, places where stones had slipped and fallen – anywhere that I might find a hand and foothold.

Another winter came and went, and then another. I grew taller, but Grandmother Pearl began to fail. More and more often she spoke in words that none of us could understand, and my brothers and my father became more and more impatient with her. Now, instead of Grandmother carrying me on her back as she had done when I was a baby, I carried her. She was so little and light that I worried about the wind picking her up and tossing her away, and I wrapped her tightly in my own felt cloak.

When we stopped to make camp, I would sit
her on the cloak as if she were a small child, and
sometimes she would smile at me and sometimes
she would stare away into the nothingness of the
sky. My brothers talked loudly now about how it
would be when they could take the herds of
horses away from the wall and into the hills.
My father did not stop them.

It was a clear spring evening when I saw the place. We had pitched the tents, and my father was checking the new foals. Soon it would be time to take the pick of them to the crossing of the river where he met other tribesmen, and the selling and bartering went on. Grandmother Pearl was half-sleeping, half-waking by the fire and I was walking beside the wall, picking sorrel to flavour our evening food. And there it was.

A deep crack, splitting the outer face from top to bottom. Bushes and shrubs had taken seed in the crevices, and almost covered the gaps and missing stones, but the cleft was wide. I walked a little nearer, and it was good. It would be hard, but I could do it.

44

Night had never taken longer to come.
My father and brothers worked with the horses
until late, and then came to the fires to eat, and
finally, sleep. Grandmother Pearl sat unmoving,
and once or twice I thought I could see the glow
of the flames shining right through her thin,
frail body.

The moon was covered in a coat of clouds, but
there were stars in the deep blue of the sky.
The fire burnt down to a steady glow, and I could
hear the sound of heavy breathing as my father
and brothers slept. Grandmother sat on by the
embers. Usually I would have helped her into her
sleeping place long before, but she made no sign
that she knew that I was late. She did not turn
as I wrapped the cloak round her and lifted her.

Chapter 5

The climb was hard. Very hard. Although Grandmother was so little I still had to hold her safe on my back with one hand, and once I thought I had lost both of us as a branch tore away beneath my feet. I caught at a root – and I was lucky that it held. I stopped for a moment to gasp for breath, and felt Grandmother's small thin arms creep round my neck and hold on tightly. She began to make a strange, sweet sound – and I realised she was singing. There were no words, only a tiny thread of sound, like the song of a dawn bird.

I took a deep breath, and went on climbing. Sweat dripped from my forehead and ran, stinging, into my eyes. I couldn't wipe it away. The moon came out from behind the clouds, and that helped me see. Up and up and up I climbed – and then, with a final heave and a gasping for breath, I was there. On the top of the wall. And Grandmother Pearl let go of me, and sang as she looked at the place where she had been born. And I realised, with a sickening lurching of my stomach, that there was no way we could ever get down the other side.

I didn't see the soldier coming. The first I knew was a heavy hand on my shoulder, and a patter of strange words. His grip was painful, and determined. I remembered my oldest brother's words. "If he's seen on the wall, it means death." And a cold terror froze me.

I'll never know what Grandmother Pearl said. She put her minute claw of a hand on the soldier's arm and looked at him with her faraway cloudy eyes, and she spoke the words I had heard her use so often when she told me of the funeral houses. And the soldier let me go. He let me go, and he put his hands together and made me a deep bow. Then he picked up Grandmother Pearl as if she was the most precious jewel in the whole wide world, and carried her away. And Grandmother Pearl sang as she went, and I knew she was singing me goodbye, and when her voice faded and stopped I knew it was her goodbye to the world as well. Grandmother Pearl had gone home to her ancestors.

My father was waiting for me as I slid and slithered back down the wall. I arrived at the bottom in a rush of little stones, and waited for his anger to break over my head. Instead, he said nothing. He put out his hand to help me up, and we walked to the tents side by side.

Job title: VILLAGE BARBER

Location: barber's shop in Pushnapanjipetal

Main work activities: shaving beards; soaping, lathering and foaming; sweeping up curls and whiskers on the shop floor; and sharpening the razor on the wetted stone

Tools: a shining silver razor

Skills and knowledge required: the art of shaving with seven swift swoops of the silver razor

Personal qualities required: ability to work hard; good manners and concentration

Appearance: well-groomed

54

Job title: PIRATE

Location: the oceans of the world

Main work activities: sailing the oceans; wrecking ships; collecting shiny objects and razing villages to the ground

Tools: a sword

Skills and knowledge required: piratical songs and terrible curses

Personal qualities required: love of water; loud growling voice and roaring laugh

Appearance: luxuriant black and curly beard, golden earring, black teeth

Ideas for guided reading

Learning objectives: understand how writers use different structures to create coherence and impact; sustain engagement with longer texts using different techniques; use the techniques of dialogic talk to explore ideas, topics or issues

Curriculum links: Geography: Passport to the world; Citizenship: Living in a diverse world

Interest words: luxuriant, piratical, illustrious, ancestor, monstrous, barricade, tedious

Resources: whiteboard, pens, paper, poster-sized paper

Getting started

This book can be read over two or more guided reading sessions.

- Read the title and blurb on the front and back covers. Discuss what a "far off land" is and name some known stories from far off lands (Aladdin, Ali Baba).

- Predict some of the features that tales from "far off lands" may contain (e.g. magical characters, unusual settings, different lifestyles).

- In small groups, ask children to read chapter 1 of *Selim-Hassan the Seventh* and chapter 1 of *The Wall*.

Reading and responding

- Discuss how authors can create impact at the beginning of magical stories (e.g. use of first person narrative, unusual language, repetition, alliteration, questions, dialogue, etc.).

- Ask children to look back over chapter 1 of each story and note the features that create impact during the opening.

- Invite children to discuss the features that the author has used and decide how effective they are at engaging the reader.